MW00559154

One Happy Chicken

Diane Calkins

Sharon Davey

ISBN 978-1-54398-062-2 (print)

Dedicated to
two kind children,
their patient father
and
Dr. Brian Loudis
who saved Zoe's life

One day a tiny brown chicken
found herself all alone on a sidewalk

A lady out for a walk scooped her up and said,
"You're adorable."

"But I can't keep you," the lady said to the tiny chick.
"Chickens are not allowed in my fancy neighborhood,
Let's find you a family!"

The very next the lady called her friend, the mother of two kind children.

"I know you already have three dogs, six cats, two small parrots and a bunny, but I found a baby chick that really needs a home."

"I guess we could take her,"
said the mom.

The dad answered the door.

"But, but, but...," said the dad.
"We already have
three dogs,
six cats,
two small parrots,
and a bunny."

However the children had already seen the chick.

"I guess we're keeping her!"

Welcome
Home
Zoe

Because Zoe was only four inches tall, she spent her days in a pen on the lawn.

And her nights

in the guest shower.

Months passed,
and Zoe became a grown-up chicken.

By that time,
she was head of the whole pack.

But Zoe wasn't the boss of Foxy,
a new foster dog.
Foxy licked Zoe like a lollipop and
chewed on her bottom.

The mom called all over town to find a vet
who could take care of a chicken.
She finally found one.

Week 1

Week 2

"She'll be good as new in a week or two," the vet said.
Zoe proudly showed off her bandage.
People stared and said,
"Look at the chicken with the big bandage on her butt."

Foxy the foster dog never bothered Zoe again.
She was adopted and went to her new home.

But that wasn't the end of Zoe's adventures.

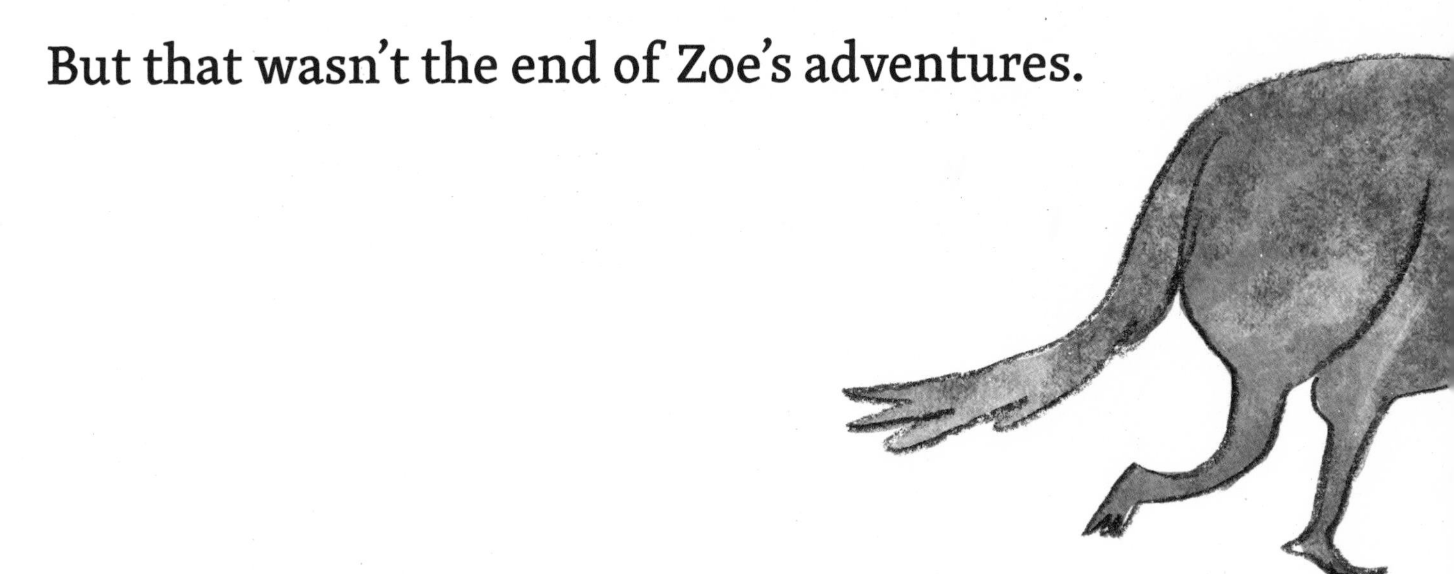

One dark and stormy night Zoe decided to sleep in a huge tree outside the fence.

The boy had to climb a tall ladder in the wind and grab the soaking wet chicken.

"We can fix that," said the vet.

He clipped her wings,
and she stayed grounded.

But Zoe didn't stay out of trouble. Instead of climbing into her special chicken coop at bedtime, she strutted along the wall crowing like a rooster.

Zoe plucked all the leaves off the rose bushes and small fruit trees.

Zoe!

NO!

"Zoe! No!," said the dad.

Then Zoe snatched all the flower bulbs the mom planted in pots.

"No Zoe," said the mom.

Zoe pecked the children's bare toes.
And when she got mad,
she grabbed a piece of skin
in her beak and twisted.
Hard.

"Zoe! That hurts!"
cried the children.

Despite her bad habits, Zoe did lay an egg every day.
But never in her special chicken coop!

She laid eggs behind the computer,
next to the coffee maker,
on the living room couch,
under a chair,
and even in the dryer.

"Surprise!" said the mom as she pulled a freshly laid egg out of the dryer

When Bonnie Beagle tried to take an egg for a snack,
Zoe chased that dog away with her wings outstretched.

“Don’t mess with Zoe.”
said the girl.
“She’s the boss
around here.”

As time passed,
the three dogs,
six cats,
two small parrots,
and bunny
grew much older.

So did Zoe.

Even the children were ready to fly the coop.
Zoe retired from egg laying and toe pecking.

Zoe spent the rest of her days eating pine nuts and grapes and clucking contentedly.

She was one happy chicken.